THIS WALKER BOOK BELONGS TO:

_____

_____

_____

banana

guava

orange

mango

pineapple

avocado pear

passion fruit

tangerine

banana

guava

orange

mango

pineapple

avocado pear

passion fruit

tangerine

For Emma, Linda, Nadine and Yewande

The author would like to thank everyone
who helped her research this book,
especially Wanjiru and Nyambura
from the Kenyan Tourist Office,
and Achieng from the Kenyan High Commission.

The children featured in this book
are from the Luo tribe of south-west Kenya.

First published 1994 by
Walker Books Ltd
87 Vauxhall Walk
London SE11 5HJ

This edition published 2006 for Bookstart

18 20 19

© 1994 Eileen Browne

This book has been typeset in Caslon 540

Printed in China

British Library Cataloguing in Publication Data:
a catalogue record for this book is
available from the British Library

ISBN-13: 978-0-7445-3634-8
ISBN-10: 0-7445-3634-0

www.walkerbooks.co.uk

HANDA'S SURPRISE

EILEEN BROWNE

WALKER BOOKS

AND SUBSIDIARIES

LONDON • BOSTON • SYDNEY • AUCKLAND

Handa put seven delicious fruits in a basket
for her friend, Akeyo.

She will be surprised, thought Handa
as she set off for Akeyo's village.

I wonder which fruit she'll like best?

Will she like the soft yellow banana ...

or the sweet-smelling guava?

Will she like the round juicy orange …

or the ripe red mango?

Will she like the spiky-leaved pineapple …

the creamy green avocado …

or the tangy purple passion-fruit?

Which fruit will Akeyo like best?

"Hello, Akeyo," said Handa. "I've brought you a surprise."

"Handa

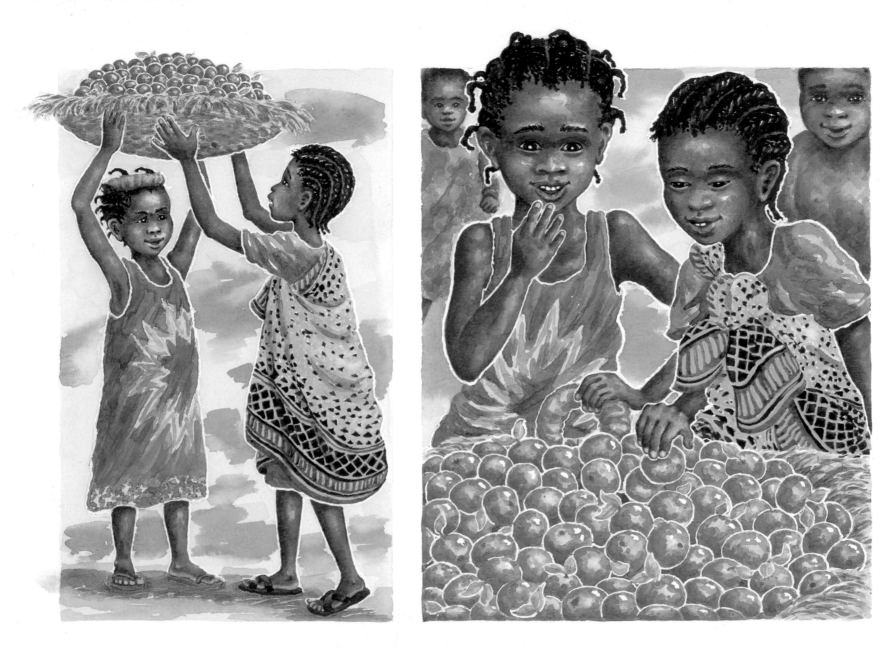

"Tangerines!" said Akeyo. "My favourite fruit."
"TANGERINES?" said Handa. "That *is* a surprise!"

monkey

ostrich

zebra

elephant

giraffe

antelope

parrot

goat

monkey

ostrich

zebra

elephant

giraffe

antelope

parrot

goat

ALSO BY EILEEN BROWNE

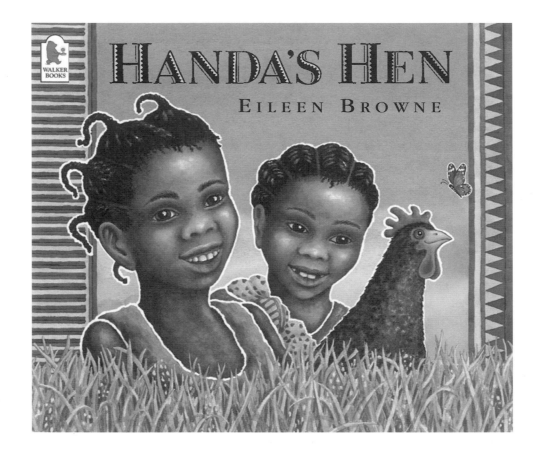